CAPTAIN PUGWASH
and the MUTINY

Also available:

Captain Pugwash
Pugwash Aloft
Pugwash and the Ghost Ship
Pugwash in the Pacific
Pugwash and the Buried Treasure
Pugwash and the Sea Monster
Pugwash the Smuggler
Captain Pugwash and the Pigwig
Captain Pugwash and the Birthday Party
Captain Pugwash and the Wreckers

CAPTAIN PUGWASH and the MUTINY

JOHN RYAN

F
FRANCES LINCOLN
CHILDREN'S BOOKS

First published in 1982 by The Bodley Head Ltd

This edition published in Great Britain in 2010 and in the USA in 2011 by
Frances Lincoln Children's Books, 4 Torriano Mews,
Torriano Avenue, London NW5 2RZ
www.franceslincoln.com

A catalogue record for this book is available from the British Library.

ISBN 978-1-84780-072-5

Printed in Croydon, Surrey, UK by CPI Bookmarque Ltd. in May 2011

3 5 7 9 8 6 4 2

Contents

Captain Pugwash and the Mutiny

A MAP
to explain the story of
CAPTAIN PUGWASH
& the MUTINY
The Wind which blew the smell towards Jake's pirates
Jake's pirates landed here
PACIFIC OCEAN

The
SLAND
N
W
E
S
er they carried
e dinghy to here
Tom's
Look-out
Rocky Point
The "Flying
Dustman"
anchored
here
Jake's pirates came
this way
e "Black Pig"
nchored here

It was quite early in the morning, and the *Black Pig* lay at anchor in the shelter of a little rocky bay, by an island far away in the blue Pacific ocean.

On any other day Captain Pugwash and his pirates would still have been fast asleep, but this morning was different. The Captain had decided to smarten up his ship and his crew. Everybody had been called early, and even Captain Pugwash was up and dressed and sitting in his cabin sipping the early morning tea which Tom the cabin boy had brought him.

He was also putting the finishing touches to a large notice which he had written out. In fact he had just signed his name at the bottom when there was a knock on his door and the Mate came in looking rather uncomfortable.

"Beggin' pardon Cap'n," said he, "but the crew 'as a complaint. The ship's biscuits is hunfit for 'uman consumption. They're full of weevils!"

"Wallopping whales! What on *earth* is a weevil?" asked the Captain.

"They're like small beetles, Cap'n," said Tom. "They eat biscuits."

"In that case," said Pugwash crossly, "the crew had better eat them quickly—or there won't be any biscuits left."

"Sorry, Cap'n, the men won't touch 'em," said the Mate. "They reckon it's cruelty to weevils!"

At this stage, the Captain became very angry.

"Doddering dolphins, Master Mate," h
cried. "Pirates should be desperadoes—no
do-gooders! Take thi
notice and nail it to th
main mast immediately
Things are going t
be very different aboar
this ship from now on!"

So the Mate took the notice and
nailed it to the mast . . .

but when Barnabas and Willy read it,
they were filled with horror and dismay . . .

and when *he* read it, so was the Mate . . .

For a time they muttered angrily together.

Then . . .

straight into the middle of the
Captain's breakfast . . .

marched the three pirates.

"Muttering midships!" cried Pugwash. "*What* is the meaning of this!"

"This", replied the Mate, "is a mutiny! *We* are taking over the ship."

"Aye," chortled Willy, "we're all captains now!"

"And you are goin' to be marooned on the island," growled Barnabas.

"Hexactly!" said the Mate. "Tom lad . . . pack up the Captain's kit and load it on the dinghy. He's leaving!"

Poor Captain Pugwash!

He muttered and spluttered a lot . . .

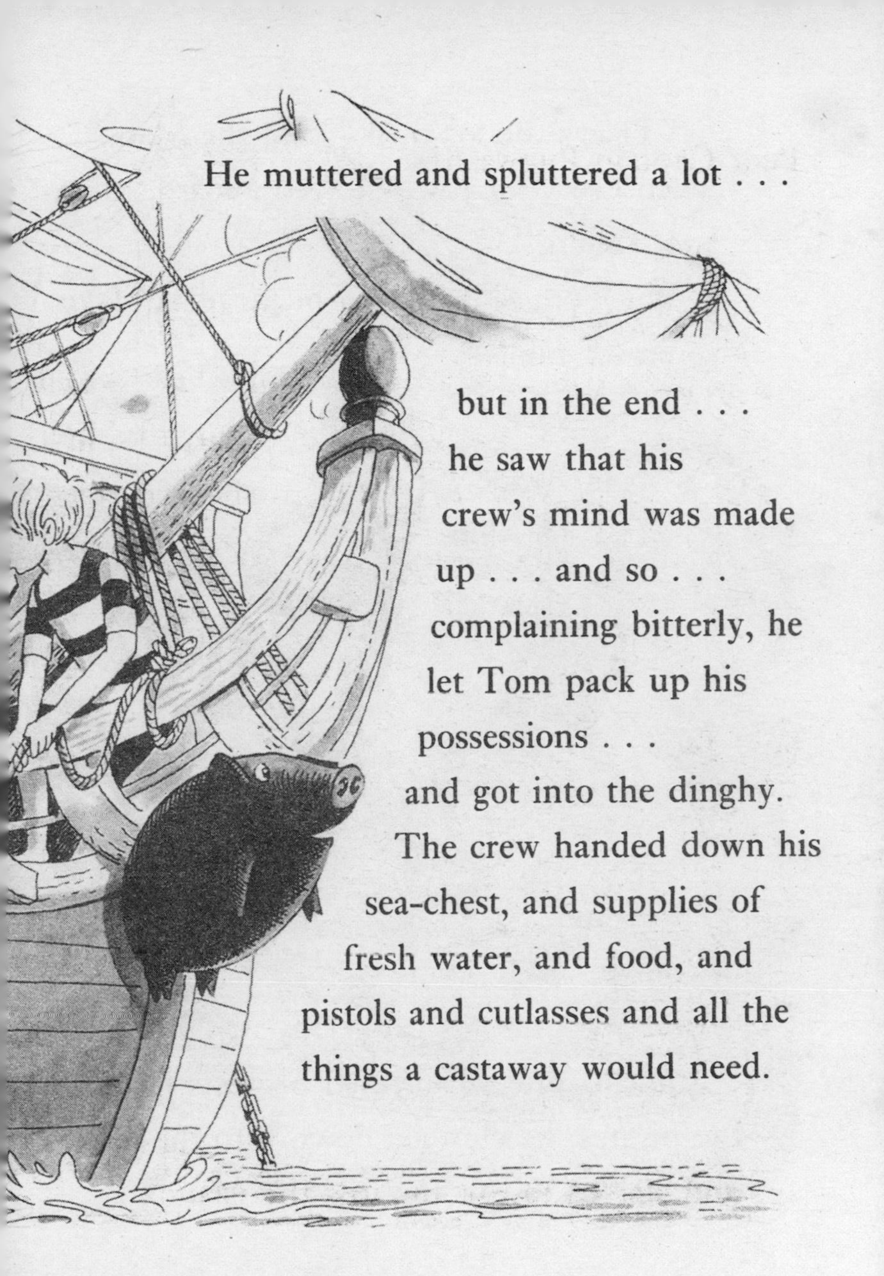

but in the end . . .
he saw that his
crew's mind was made
up . . . and so . . .
complaining bitterly, he
let Tom pack up his
possessions . . .
and got into the dinghy.
The crew handed down his
sea-chest, and supplies of
fresh water, and food, and
pistols and cutlasses and all the
things a castaway would need.

"That's the lot then," said the Mate, when everything was stowed aboard. "Bye bye, Cap'n!"

But Tom said, "Hang on, Cap'n. Make room for me!"

"For who?" asked Barnabas in a shocked voice.

"For me, of course," said Tom. "After all, I am his cabin boy . . . Bye all!"

And in spite of horrified protests from the pirates, he climbed down into the dinghy and started to row towards the island.

"Well, who would 'ave thought it?" said Pirate Willy, as they watched the little boat moving further and further away from the *Black Pig*. They weren't too worried about doing without their Captain, but losing Tom was a disaster.

Then the Mate pulled himself together. "It's no good crying over lost cabin boys," he announced. "Hoist the main sail, Cap'n Barnabas, and you Cap'n Willy, you get the anchor up. And I'll make us all a nice cup of tea!"

But Barnabas wasn't very clever with sails. He untied th wrong ropes, and a moment later, down came the whole of the main sail . . .

and the two pirates found themselves covered in a mass of heaving canvas.

Willy didn't fare much better with the anchor. While trying to work out how best to pull it up, he leant too far over,

and lost his balance and landed with a heavy splash in the warm wet water!

"Never mind," thought Willy, as he climbed up the anchor chain, "at least there'll be a nice hot cup o'tea soon."

But when he did get back on deck, and when the other two pirates had unwrapped themselves . . . the Mate shook his head sadly.

"No tea," said he. "I've just remembered . . . Tom took the kettle with him!"

For the pirates, it was the start of a very bad day.

They couldn't sail the ship without Tom to tell them what to do; they didn't know how to cook, because Tom had always done that, too. So they were reduced to eating the despised ship's biscuits, weevils and all, and that evening they climbed miserably into their unmade bunks . . . without even their bedtime cocoa to lull them to sleep.

But . . . *much*, *much* worse was to follow . . .

For that evening, unknown to anyone, *another* pirate ship had arrived at the island and dropped anchor, out of sight, around the point, in another little bay.

It was Cut-throat Jake's ship, and Cut-throat Jake was the most terrible pirate afloat, and by far Captain Pugwash's worst and most frightening enemy.

Even now, Jake and his hideous crew, with muffled oars, were setting off in their longboat to attack the *Black Pig*.

The moon was just rising and Jake rubbed his great hairy hands and growled,

"Dunno why we bothers to muffle them oars! That old rapscallion Pugwash and his useless crew will be snorin' their fat 'eads off by now. And oh-ho-ho—have they got an ugly shock comin'!"

But Jake was wrong about the Captain. Far away out of sight on the island, he and Tom were very snug. While Pugwash had spent the day pottering about on the island looking for buried treasure,

here . . .

there . . . and everywhere,

Tom had built a small hut out of bamboo and palm leaves.

Earlier that evening, he had cooked a delicious dinner, and now Captain Pugwash was savouring a fine old French brandy before going to bed.

In fact, he was just turning in for the night . . .

. . . as Jake's longboat slid silently under the bows of the *Black Pig*, and he and his men scrambled stealthily up the anchor chain to the deck.

"You take the crew, me beauties," whispered Jake with an evil grin.

"I'll handle my old friend, the Captain!"

It was indeed an ugly surprise for the Mate, Barnabas and Willy when they woke. Each opened his eyes to find a gleaming dagger at his throat, and within minutes, all three were trussed up like turkeys.

But of course, when Jake reached the Captain's cabin, there was no Captain to be seen.

"So," breathed Jake. "Hidin' is 'ee, the cowardly old blackguard! And it could be dangerous trying to seek 'im out in the dark. We'll lie up til mornin' . . . and then, ah-harrrh . . . *we'll* sniff 'im out!"

So Jake and his men kept watch over their captives and settled down to drink rum and play cards, and sing very rude sea-shanties until dawn. They had all quite forgotten that the Captain had a cabin boy called Tom.

On the island, Tom was woken early by the singing.

"Not like our lot to sing at this time o'day," he thought. "I wonder what's up?"

He set out for a high rock on the point to find out . . . and he saw quite a lot.

In the little bay on his left hand was Jake's ship. "Help," thought Tom. "I'd know the *Flying Dustman* anywhere."

Then, in the right-hand bay he saw Jake's longboat tied up alongside the *Black Pig*.

"That's bad," he said to himself. "Jake must have captured the ship! And *what* are we going to do about *that*?"

So Tom thought and thought, and then at last he had what seemed to be a good idea.

He went back to the dinghy
. . . and unpacked a
quantity of bacon and
eggs from the stores.

Then he lit a
fire back at the
camp-site, and
began to fry.

Luckily, his plan worked. The breeze carried the delicious smell of cooking out towards the *Black Pig* . . .

. . . just as Jake and his men came out on deck to begin their search for the Captain.

"So *that's* where he's skulking!" roared Jake. "Man the longboat, me handsomes. Now we'll take that old booby, Pugwash . . . *and* his breakfast!"

And greedily he and his men tumbled into their boat and set off for the island.

Meanwhile, Captain Pugwash was awoken by the sound of sizzling and the tempting smell . . .

but Tom said,

"This bacon's not for now. Quick! Help me with the dinghy!"

And a moment later, he and the Captain were carrying the little boat to the other side of the point.

B-B-BUT... WH-WHAT...
SHH, CAP'N, KEEP YOUR HEAD DOWN!

Poor Captain Pugwash. It was bad enough to have lost his ship, but now, with his breakfast gone as well he began to feel quite sorry for himself. And of course he had no idea what was *really* happening.

For, just as Cut-throat Jake was beaching his longboat on one side of the point . . .

Tom, hidden from Jake on the other side, was setting out with the Captain in the dinghy . . .

and making (to Pugwash's surprise) *not* for the *Black Pig* . . .

but for *Jake*'s ship, the *Flying Dustman*!

"Now, Cap'n," said Tom, when they reached it. "Hold tight to the anchor chain . . . I'm going to saw it through and cast the *Flying Dustman* adrift."

And very soon Tom had hacked through one of the rusty links. The chain fell away into the water, and if Tom hadn't grabbed him the Captain would have fallen in, too.

Then Tom started to row for all he was worth back towards the *Black Pig*.

In the meantime, on the island, Jake and his pirates had followed their noses to the camp-site, and were quarrelling greedily over the bacon and eggs.

In fact, they'd forgotten all about the man they were looking for . . .

until suddenly
Jake looked round
and saw . . .
to his amazement, horror and fury . . .

. . . Tom and the Captain climbing on board the *Black Pig* and his own *Flying Dustman* drifting away quite fast on the outgoing tide.

"AFTER THEM!" roared Jake, and he and his men rushed back to their longboat . . .

But by the time they were afloat Tom had untied the Mate and Willy and Barnabas and the *Black Pig* was under way.

A fresh breeze sprang up, and although Jake's pirates rowed like demons . . .

the *Black Pig* drew far ahead of them as the sails filled and she made for the open sea.

In fact, the ship's wake caught Jake's longboat, and pitched them all into the water. They cursed and swore horribly,

but with their own ship drifting far away on the horizon—there was nothing,

nothing at all that they could do about it except swim miserably back to the island.

"And now," said Tom, when he felt it was safe to hand over the steering wheel to the Captain, "it really is breakfast time. Bacon and eggs all round!"

"Hurrah!" cried the Mate.

"And no ship's biscuits," shouted Barnabas.

"Nor weevils, neither," added Willy.

"Poor little things!"

So, for the second time that morning Tom cooked the breakfast . . .

. . . and very good it was too.

"Clever lad, our Tom!" said the Mate.

"Aye . . . worth 'is weight in gold," said Willy, munching happily.

"*Almost* worth having the Cap'n back, to have Tom around!" remarked Barnabas.

But Pugwash didn't hear them.

"Fluttering flounders!" he cried, the steering wheel in one hand and a forkful of bacon in the other . . .

"You fellows didn't get very far without your famous Captain—eh! Fussing about a few mouldy biscuits indeed.

They soon needed me back when there was *real* trouble afoot! . . . eh, Tom lad? . . ."

But Tom was busy starting the washing up . . . and he just smiled, and said . . . nothing.

For Priscilla

Captain Pugwash and the Fancy-Dress Party

WELCOME TO TH

ANCY·DRESS PARTY

It was a pleasant sunny morning in a busy English sea-port. On every side was the hustle and bustle of the harbour. There were ships of every shape and size, but one in particular attracted the attention of the crowd for she had never been seen in that town before.

1680

It was Captain Pugwash's ship, the *Black Pig*.

She had sailed into the harbour the night before . . .

and although she
looked well enough
outside . . .

inside, the Captain and his crew
were in a state of deepest gloom.

It had been a bad season for pirates . . .

There was no treasure left in the treasure-chest . . .

no food in the ration-store . . .

no rum in the rum-barrel.

“There isn’t a smidge of gunpowder,” said the Mate, “nor one single cannon ball!”

But at that, the Captain brightened. “CANNON BALL!!” he cried. “A *ball* . . . a party . . . a Grand Ball . . . a Fancy-dress Ball! We’ll have one on board the ship—with a trip round the bay for good measure.

"We shall invite all the smartest and *richest* folk in town. They'll come in their finest clothes, gleaming with gold and silver . . .

dripping with diamon and gems. And once they're on board – ho-ho! – we'll put a sleeping drug in their Rum Punch . . .

then . . . hee-hee . . . as we sail round the bay, they will all fall into a deep sleep! . . .

at which point, we strip them of all their richest possessions . . . put them ashore . . . and sail away as wealthy as kings!"

The pirates all thought this was a splendid plan. Only Tom the cabin boy wasn't so sure. It seemed like daylight robbery to him . . .

But Captain Pugwash was so pleased with his plot that he actually took a gold piece (which he had pretended he hadn't got) out of his Black Piggy-Bank . . .

and gave it to the pirates to buy food and drink and bunting for the party.

Then he wrote the invitations and gave them to Tom to deliver to all the smartest addresses in town.

And it was while he was doing this . . .

that Tom noticed *someone* on the way who made him think of a quite different plan for the Captain's Party . . .
so much so that
he dropped one
invitation accidentally
on purpose on
the pavement.

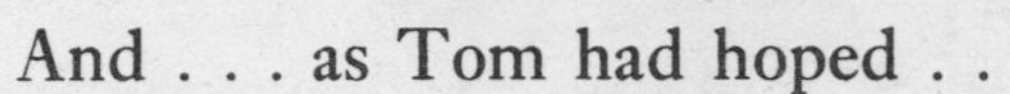

And . . . as Tom had hoped . . .

the *someone* picked
it up . . .

It was, of course, Cut-throat Jake, the Captain's worst enemy, who, with his band of wicked pirates just *happened* to be in the same town and had already observed that Pugwash was there too!

"Well, well, well," breathed Jake. "Now ain't that *real* generous of my old *friend* the Captain. A Ball on board ship . . . a trip round the Bay . . . and . . . Fancy-dress, eh?

We accept with pleasure! eh, my beauties? . . . with *much* pleasure, ho-ho-ho!"

When the morning of the Party came, Tom got out the dressing-up box. The Mate put on the uniform of a footman.

Willy disguised himself as a serving-maid.

And Barnabas did his best to look like an honest seaman.

Then:— "What about you, Cap'n?" asked Tom, for Pugwash hadn't changed at all.

"Ah!" replied the Captain, "*I'm* dressed up as a . . . guess what . . . a PIRATE CAPTAIN. Ha-ha . . . how's that for a joke?"

That afternoon, the guests began to arrive.

Everybody who was anybody was there . . . masked, be-wigged and be-jewelled . . .

and all the people of the town
gathered to watch them go aboard.

As the Mate announced the titles,

the Captain could hardly believe his good fortune!

Soon the deck was crowded with guests. Never had such a distinguished company gathered on board the *Black Pig*.

"Mix the Rum Punch, Tom!" cried the Captain. So Tom mixed it and Willy served it, and Captain Pugwash, careful to take none himself, rubbed his hands with glee at the sight of all the riches which would be his when the drink began to take effect.

Then, just as the Captain was about to give the order to sail, the Mate cried, "Wait! There's one more party to come aboard!"

And sure enough, the strangest group, wearing tall black hats and masks and cloaks held high to conceal their faces, came striding up the gang-plank.

"Maybe they'll prove the richest of the lot beneath all that disguise," thought the Captain to himself.

Then:— "Anchors aweigh!" he shouted. "Forward Miss Willy! Extra-special drinks for our mystery guests."

So Tom mixed up some more of the Rum Punch, and indeed it was extra-special. Then, as the newcomers thirstily swallowed it all up . . .

the ship sailed
out of the
harbour . . .

the crowds waved them good-bye . . .

and the guests settled down to enjoy the Ball.

Tom played merrily on his concertina, and it was not until the ship rounded the lighthouse . . .

that a terrible
voice shouted,
"UNMASK, ME
HANDSOMES!"

Then off came
the black hats
and masks, and
in a moment . . .

Pugwash and his crew and his guests
found themselves confronted and surrounded . . .

by Cut-throat Jake and his bloodthirsty band!

"Right! Grab the loot!!" roared Cut-throat Jake. His wicked eye glinted and his great black beard bristled with greed as he watched his villainous blackguards

snatching the Duchess's diamonds, the Mayor's chain of office . . .

rings, necklaces and bracelets,

silver watches and purses of gold galore!

Soon a great heap of booty lay in the middle of the deck. Jake chuckled with glee and addressed the guests.

"Much obliged, I'm sure," he growled.

"And now, in return for your – er – *generosity* – I'm goin' to set 'ee all adrift in the longboat, while *we* make our get-away in this 'ere 'andsome vessel!

"But as for *you*, you scurvy lot," he snarled, turning on Pugwash and his crew. "You what 'as contributed *nothing* to the Cut-throat Jake Benefit Fund . . .

I'll waste no longboat on *your* worthless skins! You'll walk the plank every one of you!"

And then, suddenly, even as he spoke . . .

Jake blinked, swayed and staggered . . .

and fell flat on his back in a dead faint on the deck—

and all his crew did the same!

Captain Pugwash was astonished. Why had only Jake and his men suffered from the drugged drinks?

But then he realised that all the guests were cheering, and they were cheering HIM! They didn't know, of course, that Pugwash had intended to rob *them*. They thought he'd arranged to drug Jake's drinks to save them! Least of all did they know that it was all Tom's doing!

"Bravo, Captain!" cried the Mayor. "Very quick thinking on your part!"

"Dashed fine show," said Sir Splycemeigh-Maynebrace. "The skill and speed with which you dealt with those dreadful desperadoes has saved us all!"

Then the guests recovered their stolen possessions, and the *Black Pig* sailed back into the harbour again.

And Jake and his crew, awake now, but in irons . . .

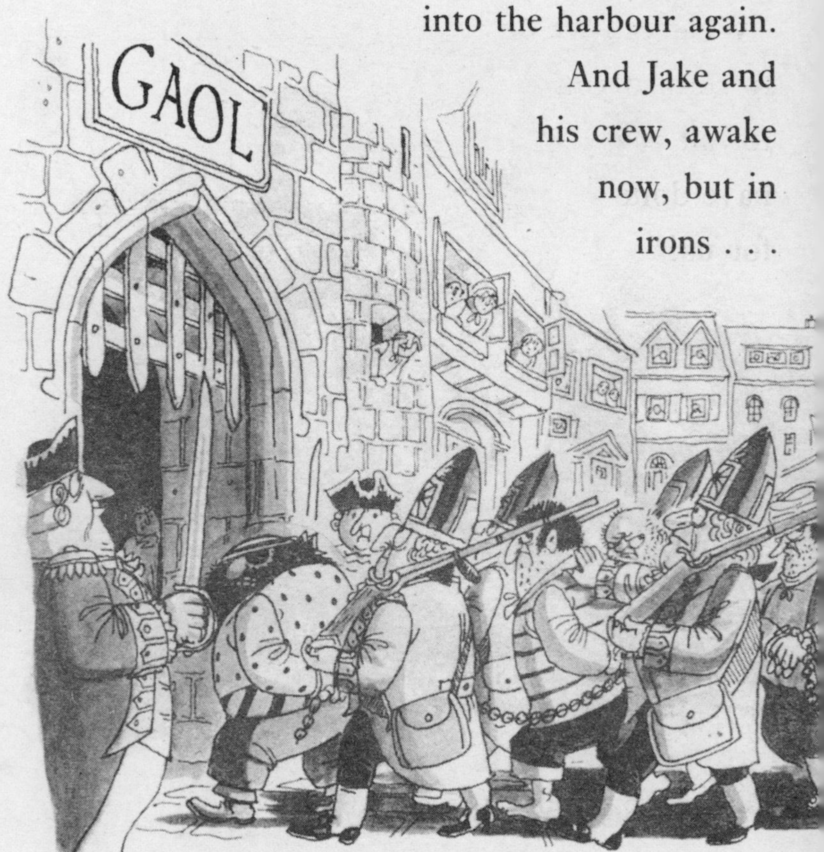

were marched away to the deepest dungeons of the town gaol.

"And now, Captain," said the Mayor when the guests had dispersed to their homes. "What can we do to reward you for all *you* have done for us?"

"Well, since you mention it, there *are* one or two little things we could do with," replied the Captain.

"A few ships' stores, perhaps. Provisions—rum, cannon balls and gunpowder so that we may set sail again and go about our honest trade!"

"It shall be done," said the Mayor.

And the next day, the Mayor himself came to supervise the delivery of all the supplies the Captain had asked for.

There was even a handsome cash present for Pugwash himself to mark the skill and presence of mind with which he had disposed of Cut-throat Jake and his band.

"Why fancy that, Captain," said the Mayor, as he shook him warmly by the hand. "You're *still* wearing your fancy-dress!"

"Suffering sea-snakes! So I am!" cried the Captain. "Young Tom ought to have reminded me! Not very bright, that cabin boy of mine!"

And Tom smiled as he listened to the Captain's remarks,

but he said nothing.

JOHN RYAN

was born in Edinburgh and spent
his early childhood in the UK and Morocco.
He worked for seven years as
Assistant Art Master of Harrow School.
Captain Pugwash first set sail over 50 years ago
as a strip cartoon. Since then he has featured in books,
films and theatres all over the world. Before his death
in 2009 aged 88, John lived in Rye, Sussex, the home
of smugglers in years gone by, with his wife Priscilla,
who is also an artist. He has three children and
a regular crew of grandchildren.